BRIDGEPORT PUBLIC LIBRARY
BRIDGEPORT PUBLIC LIBRARY
3 4000 07148 0891
W9-BRI-949

Property of
BRIDGEPORT PUBLIC LIBRARY
Newfield Branch

Tinker and Tom and the Star Baby

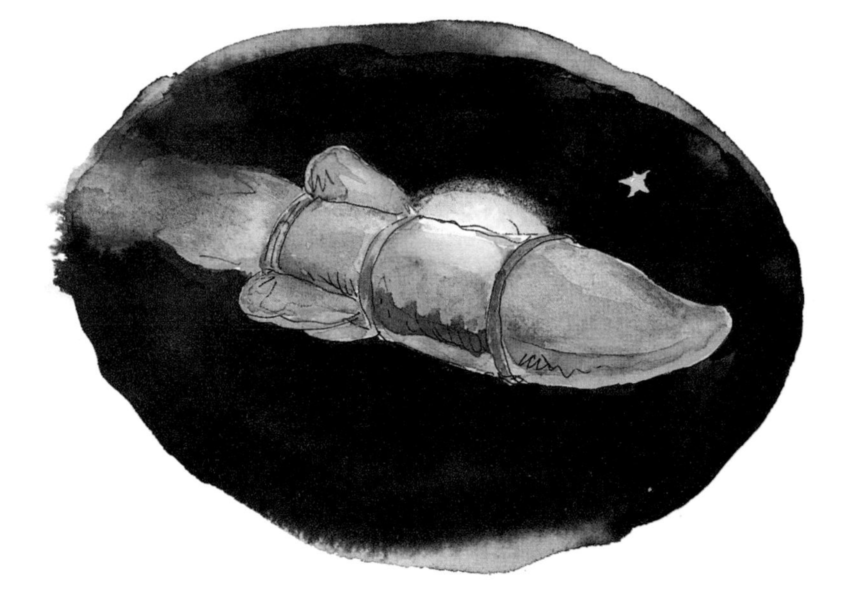

For my mom

First Edition

Library of Congress Cataloging-in-Publication Data

McPhail, David M.
Tinker and Tom and the Star Baby / David McPhail.
p. cm.
Summary: Tinker and Tom, a boy and a bear, find a Star Baby in their backyard and try to fix its spaceship so that it can return to its mother.
ISBN 0-316-56349-8
[1. Extraterrestrial beings—Fiction. 2. Bears—Fiction. 3. Science fiction.] I. Title.
PZ7.M2427Tj 1998
[E]—dc21 96-45439

10 9 8 7 6 5 4 3 2 1

NIL

Published simultaneously in Canada by Little, Brown & Company (Canada) Limited

Printed in Italy

The paintings for this book were done in watercolor and pen-and-ink on Strathmore 500 series drawing paper.

Tinker and Tom and the Star Baby

David McPhail

Little, Brown and Company
Boston New York Toronto London

Tinker and Tom couldn't get to sleep, so they sat on the edge of the bed, gazing out the window.

They had not been there long when a small, bright object went streaking through the sky.

"What's that?" gasped Tom.

"That's a baby star," Tinker told him. "It probably got lost and now it's looking for its mother."

“Well, that Star Baby must think its mother is in our backyard,” said Tom as the bright object shot past the window and disappeared over the crest of the hill in the middle of the yard.

“Quick, Tom,” said Tinker. “That Star Baby might need some help!”

Tom followed Tinker down the stairs and out through the kitchen door into the backyard.

When they reached the top of the hill, they saw it. The object that had shone so brightly only moments before now glowed ever so faintly.

"It's a spaceship!" cried Tinker.

Indeed it was . . . although it looked like a trash can with tail fins and a pointy top.

As Tinker and Tom stood looking at the little craft, they thought they heard a small voice crying.

Tom rolled the spaceship over, and when he did, a bubble-shaped lid popped open.

Inside the spaceship sat a tiny star-headed baby, and when it saw Tom's fuzzy face, it stopped crying and began to coo. Then it reached up and smiled.

"It likes me," said Tom as he picked up the baby and hugged it.
"Maybe it thinks you're its mother," said Tinker.
"I'm not your mother," Tom said, chuckling. "I'm a bear."

While Tom held the baby, Tinker examined the spaceship.
"It's got a few dents," he reported. "But nothing seems to be broken."

"Maybe it's just out of gas," suggested Tom.
"Maybe," said Tinker, "but let's take it inside for a closer look."

So Tinker and Tom carried the Star Baby and the spaceship back to the house.

In the kitchen, Tom put the baby on the floor and helped Tinker hoist the spaceship onto the table.

Then they found a couple of hammers in a drawer and began to pound out the dents.

Meanwhile, the Star Baby had discovered Fluffy the cat's food dish.

Fluffy, who had been sleeping on a pile of clean clothes, woke up and saw that the Star Baby was eating all of her food.

Fluffy hissed and prepared to pounce.
"Don't you hurt that baby!" Tinker warned the cat.

Too late.

Fluffy sprang toward the Star Baby, who just looked up and pointed at the fast-approaching cat.

Instantly Fluffy flipped over onto her back and began to float around the room.

The Star Baby kept eating and pointing, and soon Fluffy was joined in orbit by a wide assortment of things, including the toaster, the blender, and several boxes of cereal.

A few of Tinker's crayons joined the procession, making interesting designs on the walls and ceiling as they circled the room.

The pounding had awakened Tinker's father, who came downstairs to see what all the noise was about.

"What's going on down here?" he demanded.
"We're trying to fix the Star Baby's spaceship,"
Tinker explained, "so it can go and find its mother."

That's when Tinker's father caught sight of the Star Baby.

He opened his mouth to say something, but nothing came out. He could only stare and point. The Star Baby, its mouth smeared with cat food, pointed right back.

Tinker's father rose several inches off the floor, spun around three times, then drifted back up the stairs.

"Hey, Dad," Tinker called after him, "do we have any rocket fuel?"

But his father didn't answer, so Tinker decided to try and make some.

He took some orange juice from the refrigerator and poured it into a small hole he found in the rear of the spaceship.

To that he added a bottle of ketchup, a can of pea soup, a jar of honey, a pot of baked beans, a dozen or so eggs, and half a box of soap powder.

“Now let’s see if it works,” Tinker said to Tom. So they carried the spaceship and the Star Baby back outside.

Tinker set the spaceship on the ground.
"Put the Star Baby in," he said to Tom.
But Tom continued to hold the baby.

"Can't we keep it?" he groaned.

"You know we can't, Tom," said Tinker. "The Star Baby needs to find its mother."

Tom sighed. Then he gave the Star Baby one last hug and placed it gently inside the spaceship.

When Tinker closed the lid, the spaceship began to glow and hum. But it didn't budge.

"Let's give it a push," said Tinker.
So they did.

The Star Baby laughed and squealed as the spaceship went scraping and bouncing across the yard.

Then, with a bang and a whoosh, the little craft shot into the sky, leaving a wispy trail of smoke.

In a moment it was out of sight.

"Good-bye, Star Baby," called Tom.

For a long time, Tinker and Tom just stood there, looking up.

Suddenly, from far away, a beam of light shone down on them.
"I think the Star Baby has finally found its mother," said Tinker.

Then he and Tom walked slowly back to the house.